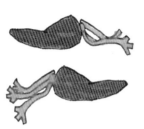

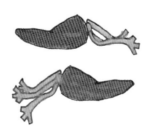

Bedtime at Bessie and Lil's

Julie Sternberg Illustrated by Adam Gudeon

BOYDS MILLS PRESS
AN IMPRINT OF HIGHLIGHTS
Honesdale, Pennsylvania

Text copyright © 2015 by Julie Sternberg
Illustrations copyright © 2015 by Adam Gudeon
All rights reserved
For information about permission to reproduce
selections from this book, contact permissions@highlights.com.

Boyds Mills Press
An Imprint of Highlights
815 Church Street
Honesdale, Pennsylvania 18431

Printed in Malaysia
ISBN: 978-1-59078-934-6
Library of Congress Control Number: 2014943968

First edition
Production by Margaret Mosomillo
Design by Robbin Gourley
The text of this book is set in Avenir LT Std.
The illustrations are done in ink and gouache, and stained and textured with tea bags.

10 9 8 7 6 5 4 3 2 1

It was bedtime at Bessie and Lil's.
Lil was snug in her mother's lap.
Bessie practiced her headstands.

Mama Rabbit opened a bedtime book—
one of her favorites from when she was a little bunny—
and began to read.

On a moonlit night,
in a cozy room,
with a comfy bed,
a mother rabbit tucked
her little bunnies in.

"I really like the word *tuck*," said Bessie.

"I'd really like you to sit down," said Mama.

"I want to say it ten times fast," said Bessie. "Tuck, tuck, tuck, tuck, tuck, tuck—"

"Can we *read*?" demanded Lil. "We're supposed to be reading."

"Lil's right," said Mama Rabbit. "Let's read."

Outside that cozy room,
with its comfy bed,
on that moonlit night,
fireflies skipped among the trees.

"*I* can skip," said Lil. "Bessie taught me. Didn't you, Bessie?"

"Yes, I did," said Bessie.

Lil hopped up and started skipping around the room.

"Remember your back knee!" called Bessie.

"Sit back down!" cried Mama.

"Bend it!" called Bessie. "Then lift it!"

"Look at me!" yelled Lil.
"I'm skipping!

I'm skipping!

I'm—"

"Bunnies!" cried Mama.
"You must be quiet!
You'll wake the baby!
Please be quiet!"

"You always say we'll wake the baby," muttered Bessie.
"Or hurt the baby, or frighten the baby, or—"

"Let's keep reading this book," said Mama Rabbit.
She began reading again.

In the cozy room,
the mother rabbit sang softly
to her sleepy little bunnies.
"Good night," she sang.
"Sleep tight," she sang.

"What's Bessie doing?" asked Lil.

"Sit down *now*, Bessie," said Mama.

"But I'm looking for fireflies," said Bessie.

"Fireflies sleep in the winter," said Mama.

"*I want to look for the moon,*" said Lil.
She jumped up to join Bessie.

Bessie put her arm around her sister.
"There it is," she said. "Between those trees."

Mama sighed. She did not ask them
to sit down again.

Instead, on that moonlit night, in that cozy room,
while one sister searched for fireflies
and the other watched the moon,
Mama Rabbit finished her bedtime story.

Then Bessie said, "Time to kiss the baby."

And Lil said, "Right! We haven't kissed the baby!"

"Oh, girls," said Mama. "Please don't wake the baby."

"We know, we know," said Bessie.

"We'll tiptoe," said Lil.

Mama closed her eyes and held her breath.
"Please, please, *please* don't wake the baby,"
she thought.
And they didn't.
They blew kisses at the baby
and tiptoed right back out.

"See?" Bessie said. "We know how to kiss the baby."

"Do you know how to kiss me?" Mama asked.

And, of course, they both did.
She kissed them back and tucked them in.

Then they lay side by side
in their comfy beds
and whispered together
and laughed together
and got shushed by Mama—
not once,
but twice—
together . . .

. . . before closing their eyes
and dreaming together
of skipping with fireflies
beneath the shimmering moon.

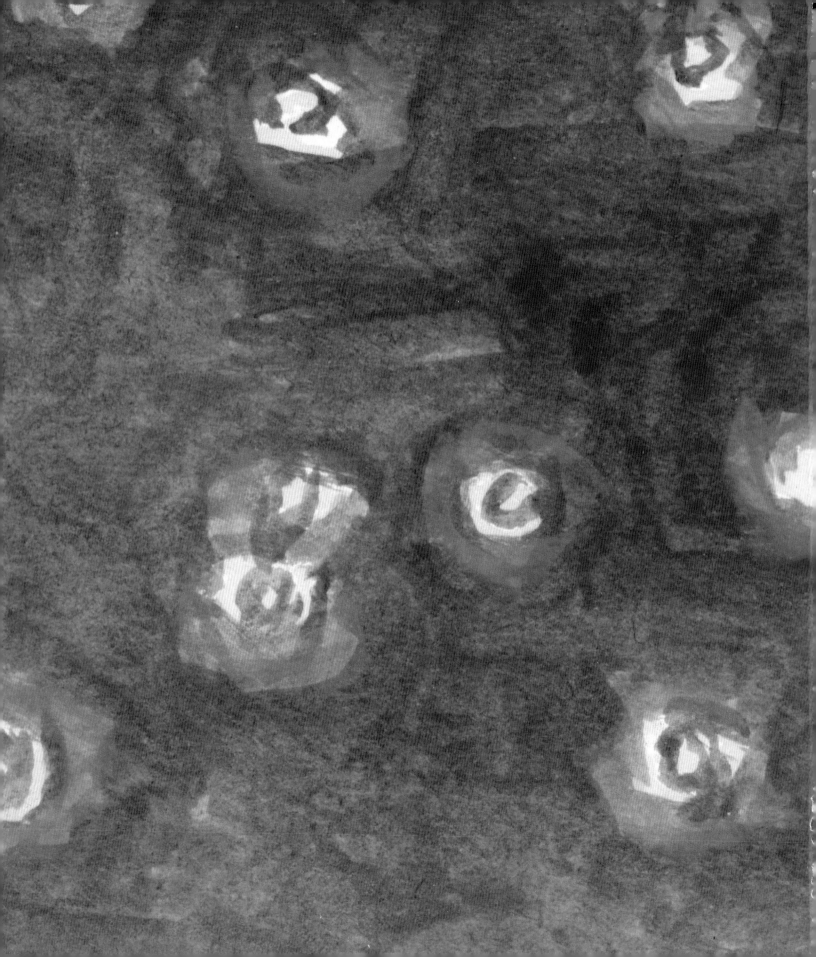